DATE DUE

FEB		JAN 2 0	2-11
DEC		JAN 28	2-11
APR		OCT 21	
MAR 5		OCT 2 5	456
MAY 1 8		FEB 17	4-6
JAN 5	E7P		
JAN 5	E7P		
MAR 2	E7P		
OCT 0			
NOV 17	SB		
DEC 1	4-D		456

Favorite Fairy Tales

TOLD IN POLAND

Favorite Fairy Tales

TOLD IN POLAND

Retold
by
VIRGINIA HAVILAND
Illustrated
by
FELIX HOFFMANN

Boston   LITTLE, BROWN AND COMPANY   Toronto

LIBRARY OF CONGRESS CATALOG CARD NO. 63-7675

Fourth Printing

These stories have been retold from the following sources:

ABOUT THE HEDGEHOG WHO BECAME PRINCE, KRENCIPAL AND
KRENCIPALKA, and ABOUT JAN THE PRINCE, PRINCESS WONDER-
FACE, AND THE FLAMEBIRD, from POLISH FAIRY BOOK by Elsie
Byrde (New York, Stokes, 1927).

THE JOLLY TAILOR WHO BECAME KING, from THE JOLLY TAILOR
AND OTHER FAIRY TALES TRANSLATED FROM THE POLISH, by
Lucia Borski (Copyright 1928 and renewed 1956, by Longmans,
Green and Company, Inc., New York).

THE LARK, THE WOLF, AND THE FOX from THE GYPSY AND THE
BEAR AND OTHER FAIRY TALES TRANSLATED FROM THE POLISH,
by Lucia Borski (Copyright 1933 and renewed 1961, by Longmans, Green and Company, Inc., New York).

THE JESTER WHO FOOLED A KING, adapted from THE MASTER
WIZARD AND OTHER POLISH TALES, by Josephine B. Bernhard and
E. Frances Le Valley, by permission of Alfred A. Knopf, Inc. Copy-
right 1934 by Josephine B. Bernhard and E. Frances Le Valley.

Published simultaneously in Canada
by Little, Brown & Company (Canada) Limited

PRINTED IN THE UNITED STATES OF AMERICA

Contents

About the Hedgehog Who Became Prince

ONCE UPON A TIME in Poland there lived a man and his wife who were jolly enough, and contented, except for one thing. No baby lay kicking in the cradle that hung from a hook in the ceiling.

The man hadn't much time to worry about this; he was busy all day in the fields. But his wife sometimes fretted about it.

One day the wife was gathering berries in the woods. Suddenly she saw a hedgehog lying under a fern. With a loud sigh she said, "Oh, if I had even a hedgehog for a baby, I would praise God."

Now the good woman did not know that Jendza the Witch was sitting in a bush near her, and had heard what she said.

Soon after this, the woman had her wish. A baby was born. But instead of having blue eyes, downy hair, and hands and feet like a human baby, this one was covered all over with sharp, prickly quills. In short, it was neither more nor less than a baby hedgehog.

"Well, I'm blessed!" said the woman. "Who would have thought that my words would come true like this! I said, 'Even if I had a hedgehog for a baby, I would praise God' — and here it is."

"Well, it is better than nothing," replied her husband. "Let us be thankful for what has come to us."

The man and his wife took good care of the little hedgehog and became fond of it. It never grew very much, and it never talked. Always it sat in the cradle.

Then one day when the woman was busy washing and felt tired, it spoke and said: "Mother, I'll take Father's dinner to him today."

And from that day everybody was surprised to

see the hedgehog carrying its father's dinner to him!

A few years later it said: "Mother, I'll take the pigs to feed in the wood."

And for the next six years this was its work. As it watched the pigs it sat under a mushroom, and never was even a single pig missing.

One day the King came riding through the wood. He had lost his way. He hunted and hunted for the path, but could not find it.

"What is Your Majesty looking for?" asked the hedgehog. The King looked round and up and down wondering where the voice came from. At

last he saw the hedgehog under the mushroom.

"I have lost my way," he replied.

"I will show it to you," said the hedgehog. "But first you must promise to give me one of your daughters in marriage."

"By all means," said the King with a polite smile. He thought to himself as he said it: It will do no harm to make this promise. Nothing will come of it.

"Your Majesty's word is not enough," said the hedgehog. "You must write it down and give me your handkerchief as a pledge."

The King was not pleased at this. He did not want a hedgehog for a son-in-law. But then he did not want to spend the night in the cold forest and be eaten by wolves, so he was obliged to write it down.

He gave the paper and the handkerchief to the hedgehog, who then guided him out of the wood. He rode back to his palace and the hedgehog took the pigs home.

A few years later, the hedgehog said: "Father, please have a saddle made for the cock, for I must ride out into the world."

A saddle was made for the cock and the hedgehog got on its back.

"Where are you going?" asked the mother.

"Don't ask me that, Mother," replied the hedgehog, and off he set on his ride into the world.

Over valley and mountain, over meadow and hill the hedgehog rode on the cock's back until they came to the palace of the King.

"What do you want?" asked the guardsman at the gate.

"I want to see the King," replied the hedgehog.

"Impossible!" said the guardsman. "The King is at dinner." But when the hedgehog showed him the King's handkerchief, he was obliged to open the gate.

What a shock for the King to have the cock come flying in with the hedgehog on its back! The

King was vexed, but a King's written word must
be kept; so he asked his three daughters which one
would consent to marry the hedgehog.

At the very idea, the Princesses nearly split
their sides with laughing. "Who ever heard of a
Princess marrying a hedgehog?" they cried.

The King flew into a rage at the hedgehog. "I'll
have you killed!" he cried, and he ordered his
guardsman to shoot the hedgehog.

At once the hedgehog gave a shrill whistle.

From every side, from near and far, hedgehogs came crawling. They came in at the windows and at the doors. They climbed up on the tables and up on the chairs. And as each one crawled by, it stuck its quills into the people near it.

Now, of course, these were not hedgehogs at all, but good fairies.

The King and Princesses, and all the Court, were hopping about with the pricks of the quills. They rubbed their legs and howled with pain.

"Stop, stop, stop!" cried the King. "You *shall* have one of my daughters!" And he commanded his youngest to marry the hedgehog.

The Princess dressed in finery and the hedgehog got on the cock's back. Thus they went to the church.

When the marriage ceremony was over, the bride turned to walk out with the bridegroom. Wonder of wonders! Instead of the hedgehog, there stood a handsome young man, who made

a low bow to the bride and offered his arm in a princely manner.

"Thank you, Princess," he said. "You have broken the spell which Jendza the Witch cast over me at my birth."

The Princess was delighted with her princely young man, and the King with his new son-in-law. The young man told them about his good parents, and they were sent for, to live near the palace. The King made his son-in-law heir to his throne.

And that night a grand ball and feast were given such as had never been enjoyed before or since.

The Jolly Tailor
Who Became King

ONCE UPON A TIME, in the town of Taida-raida, there lived a merry little tailor, Mr. Joseph Nitechka. He was a very thin man and had a small beard of one hundred and thirty-six hairs.

All tailors are thin, reminding one of a needle and thread, but Mr. Nitechka was the thinnest of all. He could pass through the eye of his own needle. He was so thin that he could eat nothing but noodles, for they were the only things which could go down his throat. But for all this, he was a very happy man, and a handsome one, too, particularly on holidays when he braided his beard.

Now Mr. Nitechka would have lived very happily in Taidaraida had it not been for a gypsy. She happened to be in the town when she cut her foot.

In her trouble she went to the tailor, who darned the skin so carefully and so neatly that not a scar could be seen. The gypsy was so grateful that she read Nitechka's future from his hand:

"If you leave this town on a Sunday and walk always westward, you will reach a place where you will be chosen King."

Nitechka laughed at this. But that very night he dreamed that he indeed became a King, and that from great prosperity he grew so fat that he looked like an immense barrel. Upon waking he thought:

"Maybe it is true — who knows? Get up, Mr. Nitechka, and go west."

He took a bundle with a hundred needles and a thousand miles of thread, a thimble, an iron, and a pair of very big scissors, and started out to find the West. He asked first one and then another in the town of Taidaraida where the West was. But no one knew. Finally he asked an old man, a hundred and six years old, who after thinking a while said:

"West must be there, where the sun sets."

This seemed so wise to Nitechka that he went that way. But he had not gone far when a gust of wind blew across the field — not a very strong gust, but, because Mr. Nitechka was so exceedingly thin, just strong enough to carry him off.

The tailor flew through the air, laughing heart-

ily at such a ride. Soon, however, the wind became tired and let him down to earth. He was much bewildered and did not come to his senses until someone shouted:

"What is this?"

Mr. Nitechka looked around and saw that he was in a wheat field and that the wind had thrown him right into the arms of a scarecrow. The scarecrow was very elegant in a blue jacket and a broken stovepipe hat, and his trousers were only a little bit torn. He had two sticks for feet and also sticks for hands.

Nitechka took off his little cap, bowed very low, and said in his thin voice:

"My regards to the honorable sir. I beg your pardon if I stepped on your foot. I am Mr. Nitechka, the tailor."

"I am pleased to meet such a charming man," answered the scarecrow. "I am Count Scarecrow, and my coat of arms is four sticks. I watch the sparrows here so that they will not steal wheat, but I give little heed to them. I am uncommonly courageous and would like to fight only with lions and tigers. This year, however, they very seldom come to eat the wheat. Where are you going, Mr. Nitechka?"

Nitechka bowed again and hopped three times, as he was very polite and knew that well-bred men greeted each other thus.

"Where do I go, Mr. Count? I am going westward to a place where I shall become King."

"Is it possible?"

"Of course! I was born to be a King. And perhaps you, Mr. Count, would like to go with me. It will be merrier."

"All right," answered the scarecrow. "I am already weary of being here. But please, Mr. Nitechka, mend my clothes a bit. I might like to marry someone on the way, and so I should be neat and handsome."

"With great pleasure!" said Nitechka. He went to work, and in an hour the scarecrow had a beau-

tiful suit and a hat almost like new. The sparrows in the field laughed at him a little, but he paid no attention to them as he walked with great dignity beside Mr. Nitechka.

On the way the two became great friends. They generally slept in a wheat field, the tailor tying himself to the scarecrow with a piece of thread so that the wind could not carry him off again. And when dogs fell upon them, the scarecrow, who was very brave because of his profession, tore out his foot and threw it after them. Then he tied it again to his body.

They continued on their way toward Pacanów, a beautiful old town, where the King had died. After seven days of adventure they reached it.

They were greatly astonished to see that all around Pacanów it was sunshiny and pleasant. But directly over Pacanów, the rain poured from the sky as from a bucket.

"I won't go in there," said the scarecrow, "because my hat will get wet."

"And even I do not wish to become King of such a wet kingdom," said the tailor.

Just then the townspeople spied them and rushed toward them, led by the burgomaster riding on a goat.

"Dear Sirs," they said, "maybe you can help us."

"And what has happened to you?" asked Nitechka.

"Deluge and destruction threaten us. Our King died a week ago, and since that time a terrible rain has come down upon our gorgeous town. We can't even make fires in our houses, because so much water runs through the chimneys. We will perish, honorable sirs!"

"It is too bad," said Nitechka very wisely.

"Oh, very bad! And we are most sorry for the late King's daughter. The poor thing can't stop crying, and this causes even more water."

"That makes it still worse," replied Nitechka, still more wisely.

"Help us, help us!" continued the burgomaster. "Do you know the immeasurable reward the Princess promises to the one who stops the rain? She promises to marry him, and then he will become King."

"Truly?" cried Nitechka. "Count Scarecrow, let's go to the town. We ought to try to help them."

Through the terrible rain they were led to the Princess. Upon seeing Nitechka, she cried out:

"Oh, what a handsome youth!"

He hopped three times and said:

"Is it true, Princess, that you will marry the one who stops the rain?"

"I vowed I would."

"And if I do it?"

"I will keep my promise."

"And I shall become a King?"

"You will, O beautiful youth."

"Very well," answered the tailor. "I am going to stop the rain."

So saying, he nodded to Count Scarecrow and they left the Princess.

The whole population, full of hope, gathered around them.

Nitechka and the scarecrow stood under an umbrella and whispered to each other:

"Listen, Scarecrow, what shall we do to make the rain stop falling?"

"We have to bring back pleasant weather."

"But how?"

"Ha! Let's think!"

But for three days they thought and the rain fell and fell and fell. Suddenly Nitechka gave a cry of joy like a goat's bleating.

"I know where the rain comes from!"

"Where from?"

"From the sky!"

"Eh!" grumbled the scarecrow. "I know that too. Surely it doesn't fall from the bottom to the top, but the other way around."

"Yes," said Nitechka, "but why does it always

fall over the town only, and not ever elsewhere?"

"Because elsewhere there is nice weather."

"You're stupid, Mr. Count," said the tailor. "But tell me, how long has it rained?"

"They say since the King died."

"You see! Now I know everything! The King was so great and mighty that when he died and went to heaven he made a huge hole in the sky."

"Oh, oh, true!"

"Through the hole the rain poured and it will pour until the end of the world if the hole isn't sewed up!"

Count Scarecrow looked at him in amazement.

"In all my life I have never seen such a wise tailor," said he.

They rejoiced greatly, went to the burgomaster, and ordered him to tell the townspeople that Mr. Joseph Nitechka, a citizen of the town of Taidaraida, had promised to stop the rain.

"Long live Mr. Nitechka! Long may he live!" shouted the whole town.

Nitechka ordered them to bring all the ladders in the town, tie them together, and lean them against the sky. He took a hundred needles and, threading one, went up the ladders. Count Scarecrow stayed at the bottom and unwound the spool on which there were a hundred miles of thread.

When Nitechka got to the very top he saw that there was a huge hole in the sky, a hole as big as the town. A torn piece of the sky hung down, and through this hole the water poured.

So he went to work and sewed and sewed for two days. His fingers grew stiff and he became very tired, but he did not stop. When he had finished sewing he pressed out the sky with the iron and then, exhausted, went down the ladders.

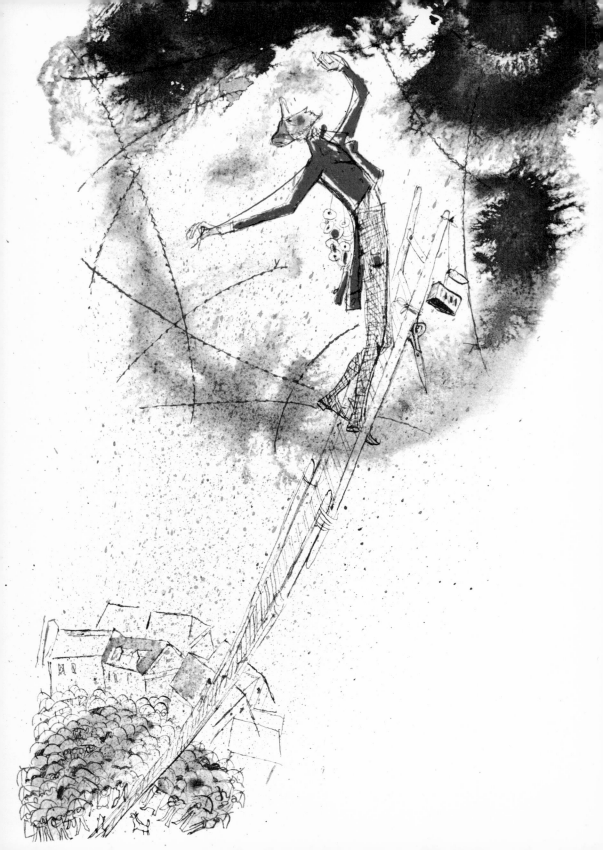

Once more the sun shone over Pacanów. Count Scarecrow almost went mad with joy, as did all the other inhabitants of the town. The Princess wiped her eyes that were almost cried out. Throwing herself on Nitechka's neck, she kissed him affectionately.

Nitechka was very happy. He looked around. There were the burgomaster and councilmen bringing him a golden scepter and a gorgeous crown, and shouting:

"Long live King Nitechka! Long live he! Long live he! And let him be the Princess's husband, and let him reign happily!"

So the merry little tailor reigned happily for a long time, and the rain never fell in his kingdom. In his good fortune Nitechka did not forget his old friend, Count Scarecrow. He appointed him the Great Warden of the Kingdom, to drive away the sparrows from the royal head.

Krencipal and Krencipalka

KRENCIPAL AND KRENCIPALKA had not a penny to bless themselves with. Their cottage was tumbling to pieces, and there was not a bite of bread in the cupboard. A bad state of things, to be sure!

"Let us go out into the world and seek our fortunes," said Krencipal to Krencipalka. So off they started.

They walked and walked, till they met a needle.

"Where are you off to?" asked the needle.

"Into the world to seek our fortune," said Krencipal and Krencipalka. And the needle said:

> *"Take me with you all the way;*
> *I will help you night and day."*

"But how are we going to carry you?" asked Krencipal and Krencipalka.

"Just stick me in your hat," answered the needle. And they did so.

They walked and walked till they met a lobster.

"Where are you off to?" asked the lobster.

"Into the world to seek our fortune," said Krencipal and Krencipalka. And the lobster said:

> *"Take me with you all the way;*
> *I will help you night and day."*

"But how are we going to carry you?" asked Krencipal and Krencipalka.

"Just put me in your basket," answered the lobster. And they did so.

They walked and walked till they met a duck.

"Where are you off to?" asked the duck.

"Into the world to seek our fortune," said Krencipal and Krencipalka. And the duck said:

"Take me with you all the way;
I will help you night and day."

"But how are we going to carry you?" asked Krencipal and Krencipalka.

"Just put me in your sack," answered the duck. And they did so.

They walked and walked till they met a cock.

"Where are you off to?" asked the cock.

"Into the world to seek our fortune," said Krencipal and Krencipalka. And the cock said:

"Take me with you all the way;
I will help you night and day."

"But how are we going to carry you?" asked Krencipal and Krencipalka.

"Just put me in with the duck," answered the cock. And they did so.

And they walked and walked till they met a pig.

"Where are you off to?" asked the pig.

"Into the world to seek our fortune," said Krencipal and Krencipalka. And the pig said:

> *"Take me with you all the way;*
> *I will help you night and day."*

"But how are we going to carry you?" asked Krencipal and Krencipalka.

"You don't need to carry me," answered the pig. "Just drive me in front of you." And they did so.

They walked and walked till they met an ox.

"Where are you off to?" asked the ox.

"Into the world to seek our fortune," said Krencipal and Krencipalka. And the ox said:

> *"Take me with you all the way;*
> *I will help you night and day."*

"Likely we're going to carry *you!*" said Krencipal and Krencipalka.

"You don't need to carry me," answered the ox. "I'll carry your wife and the basket as well." And he did so.

They walked and walked till they met a horse.

"Where are you off to?" asked the horse.

"Into the world to seek our fortune," said Krencipal and Krencipalka. And the horse said:

> *"Take me with you all the way;*
> *I will help you night and day."*

"Likely we're going to carry *you!*" said Krencipal and Krencipalka.

"You don't need to carry me," answered the horse. "I'll carry you and the sack as well." And he did so.

So Krencipal sat on the horse, Krencipalka sat on the ox, the basket was hung on the ox's horns, the sack was hung on the horse's tail, and the pig ran on in front. And they walked and walked till they came to a wood.

In this wood was a fine house in which no good

soul would live, for it was inhabited by a wicked goblin.

Krencipal and Krencipalka went into the house, the horse went into the stable, the ox went into the barn, the pig went into the sty, the cock went into the parlor, the duck went behind the kitchen stove, the lobster went into a bucket of water, and the needle went, eye downwards, into a bench in front of the table.

The pig told them to put some acorns to roast for him, and they did so.

After a while in came the goblin.

"What are you doing here, Krencipal and Krencipalka?" he asked.

"We are just passing the night here," they replied. "Pray sit down." He did so. And the needle ran into him, for he had seated himself upon the bench.

"Oh, oh, oh!" cried the goblin, and ran to the bucket of water to bathe the pricked place. But when he put his hand into the bucket the lobster seized it and squeezed it until the bones cracked.

"Oh, oh, oh!" cried the goblin, and ran to the fire for ashes to rub on his hand. But the acorns went *bang-bang-bang!* and flew out and hit him in the eye.

"Eh, eh, eh!" cried the goblin, and ran to the barn for some straw that he might wipe his eye.

But the ox caught him on its horns and threw him over its head into the stable, where the horse was standing. Then the horse let out with his hind legs and sent the goblin flying through the yard into the kitchen and out by the front door. As he passed, the duck said "Quack, quack, quack, quack, qua-ack" and the cock said "Tuck, tuck, tuck, tuck, tu-uck."

The goblin took to his heels and ran as fast as he could to the Underworld.

"What are you doing here?" asked his friends. "Why are you not at home?"

"H-o-me?" cried the goblin, his teeth chattering so that he could hardly speak. "N-n-n-ever a-g-g-ain!" He sat down to get over his fright, but it was some time before his teeth stood still enough for him to tell them what had happened.

"My house is haunted by humans," he said, as soon as he could speak. "I found two of them sitting at the table, and they asked me to take a bit of dinner with them. So I sat down on the bench, and the cook was crouched under the table and ran a skewer into me. I went to get some water to bathe the pricked place and there was a tinker sitting in the bucket who pinched my hand so hard with his pincers that the bones cracked. I went to the fire to get some ashes to rub my hand with, and there was a soldier who shot at me — *bang-bang-bang!* — and hit me clean in the eye.

"I went to the barn for some straw to wipe my eye, and there was a haymaker who tossed me up in the air with his pitchfork and right over into the stable! And there was a blacksmith who gave me such a knock with his hammer that I went flying through the yard, into the kitchen and out by the front door. As I passed, another of these creatures called, 'Smack-smack-smack-smack-smack-him w-e-ll!' and another 'Chuck-chuck-chuck-chuck-chuck-him o-u-t!' I'll never go home again!"

So Krencipal and Krencipalka stayed on in the fine house and lived there happily ever after.

The Lark, the Wolf,
and the Fox

A LARK was very much pleased with himself and the world around him. His young ones grew nicely in their nest in the low bush at the edge of the forest. He sang gaily, flying high up to the sun, then down again swiftly like a bullet.

As the lark was flying around his nest, he noticed the ground nearby quivering strangely. He stopped to watch it. Soon an opening was made and a mole came forth.

The lark sensed danger, and asked the mole: "What are you doing?"

The mole shrugged his shoulders in disdain and answered: "What a question! I burrow."

"Yes, yes. You burrow, but which way?"

"I burrow straight ahead toward that bush."

The lark almost fainted on hearing this, for right there was his nest with the young birds. He started to explain that if the mole burrowed under the bush, he would undermine the nest and kill the baby larks. The rest of the field was free; wouldn't the mole please burrow there? The lark begged and prayed and finally threatened, but the mole would not change his course. He did not care whether or not he killed the young birds. He advised the lark to move somewhere else and build a new nest.

The lark wailed loudly in despair and flew to the village to ask for help. He knew there was no use asking people. They were always ready to harm instead of help. He tried to ask the dogs, but the dogs were busy chasing the squealing pigs and did not hear his lamentations.

The cat, sleeping in the sun on a threshold, would have been glad to help, but the lark knew the cat's fondness for birds and left him alone.

The lark next flew into a barn, where the cock was busy stealing grain. Hearing the lark's voice, the cock took it for his master's and ran away with a loud *kuku-ryku!*

Outside the barn, on the roof, a flock of sparrows chirped and quarreled, paying no attention to the lark's distress.

The lark caught sight of the geese and flew to them, but they were too busy doing damage to the orchard. He heard a quail in the wheat field and flew to her, but she was playing with a little boy, making him chase her over the field.

The lark wept and cried loudly. He flew through a wood and perched on a birch tree. A wolf came out of the bushes and called angrily:

"Why do you shout and do not let decent folk sleep?"

"Oh, my dear, such a misfortune! How can I not weep?"

"*My dear*'! I like that. Well, tell me why do you cry, *my dear?*"

The lark told the wolf of his nest and the mole, and of his vain search for help.

The wolf was not particularly interested in the lark's young ones, but having nothing else to do, he said: "Well, I might help you, but I should like to eat first, for I am very hungry, really very hungry indeed."

"Oh, help me, please, help me!" cried the lark. "I'll give you plenty to eat, all you want, but you must help me."

"You, a lark, will give me food? Well, it is worth trying," said the wolf. And he followed the lark.

They went to the forester's house, where a wedding was being celebrated with a great party.

Quietly the lark and the wolf stole under an open window and listened to the singing. "Just in time," whispered the lark. "You wait here and watch for your chance."

Inside the cottage the guests were sitting down at the table, on which the housewife had placed the food on large platters. The lark flew into the room with a loud flapping of his wings and kept on flying around madly.

Everyone tried to catch the lark, but he was too quick. He flew out of the open door with all the party following him.

The lark chased them back and forth, around and around the cottage, while the wolf went in and helped himself to the food: sausages and dumplings and roasts — he ate so much that he was barely able to jump out through the window and steal away from the cottage.

Seeing the wolf again, the lark rose so high in the air that the people lost sight of her. They stood and waited; then, ashamed, went back to the cottage. What happened then, inside the cottage, the lark and the wolf did not bother their heads about.

The lark asked the wolf: "Have you eaten?"

"Oh, yes indeed! But now I should like a drink."

"Then come along."

They went to a road where an innkeeper and his son were driving a wagon with barrels of beer to the forester's wedding. The lark perched on the wagon. The innkeeper slowly stretched out his hand to catch the lark, but the bird jumped on a barrel. The innkeeper threw his cap at him, and the lark flew up and came down on his head.

"Sit quietly, I'll catch him," called the boy.

All in vain. The lark flew from the head to the whip, from the whip to the wagon, from the wagon again to a barrel. The boy lost his patience, caught a stone, and threw it . . . straight into a barrel. A stave broke, and the beer came running out. The father grew angry. He caught up the whip to strike his son.

Away ran the boy, with his father after him, while the wolf leaped upon the wagon and drank the beer from the broken barrel. He drank and drank, until he could drink no more, and slowly dragged himself to the wood.

The lark flew toward him, asking, "Have you drunk?"

"Oh, I surely have. But now I should like amusement to make me laugh a little."

"Come along then, I'll give you amusement."

They went to the manor barn, where the men

were threshing and the women were binding straw. The lark lit on a thresher's head, then flew to a woman. All stopped their work and began to chase the lark with their hats, caps, and kerchiefs. What laughter and shrieks! The fieldkeeper came hurrying to see what had caused the disturbance and the stopping of work. When the lark brushed against his nose, he, too, joined the chase. Soon the land-steward ran shouting from afar, to stop the commotion and the noise.

But, instead, he also began to chase the lark, breathlessly.

The wolf laughed and laughed so hard that he rolled on the ground with tears running down from his eyes. After a while he called to the bird:

"Enough, enough! Stop! I cannot laugh any more!"

The lark left the dumfounded people and, returning to the wood together with the wolf, asked:

"Have you amused yourself?"

"Have I? Never in my life have I laughed so

hard, my dear. But now, let us go to the mole."

They proceeded to the lark's nest, which was still intact and safe, but the ground nearby was quivering.

"Never mind," said the wolf. "You have done your part, and now I shall do mine."

He sat down beside the moving soil and watched. Soon the mole made an opening in the ground and came out, shaking earth off his fur. The wolf grabbed the mole by his neck and finished him on the spot.

"Now you shall have peace," said the wolf to the lark, going to his den to sleep.

The lark, being very grateful indeed, sang loud praises to the wolf.

Now the fox, who had his hole near the wolf's den, listened to the song of praise and almost burst with envy. He made his way noiselessly to the wolf's hole to sneer at him. But he was so astounded to find him so fat, after the forester's wedding feast, that instead of sneering he asked humbly:

"Where did you gain so much flesh, Mr. Wolf?"

"At a wedding. I was invited there and received most kindly. At no other place have I seen so much food and drink."

The fox sighed and turned yet more yellow with envy, for he had had nothing to eat in three days except an old partridge. He inquired in a roundabout way who had been so hospitable to him. The wolf pretended not to notice the intentions of the fox. He wanted to play a trick on him, for they had old accounts to settle. So, he told him of the forester's, of the number of geese and ducks there, and how easy it was to reach them.

The fox could wait no longer. He scuttled away to the forest and did not even try to conceal himself, being assured by the wolf of a welcome. But that did he not receive! All were sure that it was the fox who had eaten up their wedding feast. Now they ran after him with sticks and brooms and pokers, and beat him so hard that he barely escaped with his life.

It took weeks for the fox to recover, and his hatred for the wolf grew ever more bitter. He waited only for the chance to repay him.

Soon enough winter came and with it cold and hunger. Nothing was to be found to eat, not even the sole of an old shoe.

One day the wolf met the fox, but he was so hungry that he paid no attention to his enemy. The fox, though starved himself, rejoiced at the wolf's misery and greeted him in a sweet voice:

"You seem to be sad, Mr. Wolf."

"Do not provoke me. I am angry."

"I would ask you to have some fish, Mr. Wolf, but I dare not."

"Let me have the fish," growled the wolf, gnashing his teeth with hunger.

"The fish are in the pond nearby, they have but to be caught."

"Let us go to them, then."

The fox led the wolf to the pond, to the ice-hole where the village men caught their fish. He told the wolf to let his tail down into the water for the fish to attach themselves. He explained that as he himself had been coming here every day, the fish by now knew his tail and would bite no more. The wolf was to keep his tail in the water until it felt heavy.

After a while the wolf tried to pull up his tail. As he was able to move it, he said that it was not heavy.

"You sit here until it feels very heavy, while I fetch a basket," said the fox, going away.

The wolf sat on the ice with his tail in the ice-hole, and as there was a biting frost that day, he soon froze to the spot. Unable to move, he waited for the fox to help him lift the fish.

The fox, traitor that he was, ran to the village, shouting at every door:

"Thief! Fish! Fish! Thief!"

The people, anxious for their property, caught in their hands whatever came first — sticks, hoes and rakes — and they hastened to the pond. When

they saw the wolf, they grew yet more angry and ran at him. The wolf knew his danger and tried to get away. He struggled and pulled and tugged, but some force held him fast.

How the men did beat him! The wolf had been freezing before, but now he grew hot as the men kept on beating him. Somehow, at last, he managed to pull away, but leaving his tail behind him.

The fox, well hidden in the wood, kept on saying to himself:

"Now you have it for the forester's cottage! Now you have it for my aching sides!"

The wolf in his shame sought shelter and secrecy in the dense forest. But the fox took every opportunity to tell each creature in the wood about the wolf's fishing, and he was wise enough to move away before the wolf had time to recover. Indeed, when the wolf returned, he tried to find the fox, but he could not.

About Jan the Prince,
Princess Wonderface,
and the Flamebird

MANY YEARS AGO there lived a rich King who had three sons. The two elder were clever young men, but the youngest, Jan, was looked upon as a simpleton.

The King had many valuable possessions. One of them was a wonder-garden. Everything that grew there was beautiful, but the most beautiful of all was a silver apple tree which bore golden apples.

The King was so proud of this tree that he visited it every day. He would gaze at the apples, count them, touch them one by one, and gloat over their beauty.

One day when he went into the garden the sight of the tree made him stand still as if suddenly he had been struck by lightning. One of the apples had disappeared! The King was in despair. He called his three sons to him and said: "Whichever one of you catches the thief who has robbed my apple tree shall become my favorite and I will make him my heir."

The two elder sons stood forth and cried as if with one voice: "King and Father, your will shall be done this very day."

"And what say you, my youngest son?" asked the King of Jan the Prince, who stood silently behind his brothers.

"Nothing, Father," answered Jan.

"Simpleton!" cried his father, frowning fiercely.

That same day the eldest son feasted with his friends and boasted that he would catch the thief and inherit the kingdom. But by the time he went into the garden to watch for the thief, he felt stupid with too much food and drink. After a few minutes he lay down under the tree and fell asleep.

When he awoke, it was morning — and another apple was missing.

The next day the second son feasted with his friends. Like his brother, he boasted loudly that he was going to catch the thief and win his father's favor. But he, too, being overfull, lay down after a short watch and fell asleep. When he awoke, it was morning — and one more apple was missing.

The third night Jan, the youngest Prince, took his place quietly under the tree and watched.

Nothing happened until midnight. Then in the far east Jan spied something flaming bright fly out of a cloud. It flew nearer and nearer until at last it lighted on the tree. Jan saw that it was a brilliant bird with feathers that shone like the sun at the brightest time of day.

The bird was about to take an apple when Jan seized it by the tail. It managed to fly away, but it left one radiant feather in the Prince's hand. Jan hid the feather in his jacket, lay down and rested until dawn. Then he rose and went to the palace. As soon as he drew forth the feather, the whole palace and its court were filled with a bright light.

The King was overjoyed. "Why, it is the Flame-

bird's feather!" he cried. He then issued an edict:

> *"Whoever brings to me*
> *The spoiler of this tree*
> *Whether he be my son*
> *Or any other one*
> *The same shall be my heir*
> *And shall my kingdom share."*

From all parts of the world arrived knights, lords, and gentlemen. They kept watch day and night for many months, but the Flamebird came no more. Finally the nobles rode off in different directions seeking and inquiring after the bird.

Among them rode the two elder Princes mounted on two beautiful horses, and Jan on a slow-going nag that stumbled at every step. They rode together for a long way until they came to a crossroad. Here rose a tall cross on which was written:

> *"For him who goes straight*
> *A stick lies in wait;*

Who goes to the right
Will end in a plight;
Who takes the left way
Will oft go astray
But at last get the best of his brothers."

Now the eldest brother was just going straight on and the second was turning to the right, leaving Jan the left road, when suddenly, out from behind a hill, a wolf appeared.

This was no ordinary wolf, but a wonder-wolf. He was so thin and starved-looking that he seemed but skin and bones.

The two eldest brothers shot at him. Whether they had forgotten to load their guns or whether they missed him, the wolf stood unharmed. He howled at them and ground his teeth, and he looked so hungry that Jan felt sorry for him. All the food in his knapsack he threw to the poor beast. But his brothers went on.

The wonder-wolf then spoke in a human voice: "Thank you, O Prince. You will not regret having fed me. Just tell me where you want to go and why you want to go there."

Jan told him the whole story. When he had finished, the wolf said: "Know, O Prince, that I am no ordinary wolf. I am called the wind-wolf, for I can fly as fast as the wind. Get on my back and hold me fast round the neck. But, whatever you do, don't kick my sides or I'll eat you up."

Prince Jan did as he was told, and in a wag of a tail they were off.

Over meadows and forests, over rivers and hills, over deep seas and mountains they flew and they flew till they drew near the Far North. They stopped before a high wall.

"Here we are," said the wolf. "The Flamebird is in a garden on the other side of this wall. You must go in and take it. But I warn you not to take the cage, though it may seem to you more beautiful than the bird itself."

With that the wind-wolf flew away. The Prince jumped over the wall and saw the Flamebird sit-

ting in a cage in the center of a beautiful garden.
As he went over to take the bird, he noticed that
the cage was set with precious stones. It aroused
his admiration to such a pitch he forgot — alas! —
the warning of the wind-wolf. As he took hold

of the cage, he made a cord attached to it start a loud bell ringing. A guard came running into the garden. He seized Jan and took him before the King who owned the garden and the bird.

"And who may you be?" asked the King in a fury.

Jan replied: "I am the son of the King in whose garden grows the silver tree which bears golden apples. I needed to take the bird because he has robbed my father's tree of apples."

"It is lucky for you," said the King, "that he is your father. Because I bear him great respect, I will spare your life. I will even give you the Flamebird, but you must do something for me in return. . . .

"In a certain kingdom there reigns a King who owns a horse with a golden mane. This steed runs faster than any hare. If you will bring him here, you shall have the Flamebird, cage and all."

Jan became sad, for he had no idea how to get the horse. He went from the garden into the green fields beyond, and sat down, and began to weep.

Suddenly he heard a rumbling sound in the air. It was the wind-wolf flying towards him.

"Why do you weep?" asked the wolf.

"Alas!" cried Jan. "I have been so near happiness, and lost it!" He told the wind-wolf all that had happened.

"Foolish Prince!" said the wolf. "But I will help you again. I know that the horse with the golden mane stands in a stable with twelve locked doors. It is far away, in a land beyond the sea, but he shall be yours today. Jump on my back again and hold me fast round the neck. Whatever you do, don't kick my sides or I'll eat you up."

In a wink of the eye they were off.

Over meadows and forests, over rivers and hills, over deep seas and mountains they flew and they flew, till they drew near the West. They stopped before a high wall.

The wolf gave Jan two plants. The first was dream-grass, with which he was to put the guard

to sleep. The second was the break-lock plant, with which he was to open the twelve doors.

"But remember, Prince Jan, do not take the horse's bridle. If you do, you will be caught."

The wind-wolf flew away and Jan jumped over the wall. He waved the dream-grass over the guard until the man dropped down in a deep sleep. Then he waved the break-lock plant before the first door till the lock fell out and the door opened. He did the same before the second and third doors, and so on till all twelve doors stood wide open and the horse was within his reach.

The bridle of the golden-maned horse was studded with precious gems and was so beautiful that it made Jan forget the wind-wolf's warning. As he touched the bridle, a string attached to it set a loud bell to ringing. The guard woke up at once. He seized the Prince and took him before the King of the country. This King, too, was angry, but when Jan had told him the whole story he said:

"I will spare your life — but on one condition. In a far-off land beyond the seven seas there lives a beautiful maiden named the Princess Wonderface. You must bring her to me and I will give you not only the golden-maned horse but his bridle."

Jan was in despair. Again he went out into the green fields and wept.

Suddenly there was the rumbling sound in the air and the wolf appeared.

"What!" he exclaimed. "Weeping again? What is the matter now?"

"Matter enough," said Jan the Prince. And he told the wind-wolf all that had happened.

"Ah, foolish one!" said the wolf. "When will you learn? But I will help you again, for I know how to find the Princess Wonderface. Jump on my back as before. Hold tight, and don't kick my sides or I'll eat you up."

In a snap of the jaws they were off.

Over meadows and forests, over rivers and hills, over deep seas and mountains they flew and flew till they drew near the South. Now they stopped outside a palace wall.

"On the other side of this wall there is a garden, and there walks the Princess Wonderface," said the wolf. "Wait you here and I will fetch her for you."

So saying, the wolf stamped on the ground. He turned into a splendid young Prince, and at once jumped over the wall. The Princess Wonderface was walking there with her maidens. She thought he must be a guest come to see her father, and talked to him pleasantly. But all at once he seized her round the waist and jumped with her back over the palace wall. He then turned back into a wolf and he with Jan and the Princess went on their way.

The Princess quickly came out of the fainting spell into which she had fallen. As soon as she looked upon Jan, she fell in love with him and he with her, for they were both young and beautiful. She broke in two a precious ring she was wearing; she gave one half to the Prince as a token and kept the other half herself.

Their journey was very happy, but — alas! — in time they reached the palace of the King to whom Jan was to bring the Princess. At the thought of parting, they were both full of grief. What was to be done? They began to weep bitterly.

The wolf saw them and said: "Now, dry your eyes. You shall not part from each other. I can help you. I will turn myself into a Princess and the Prince shall take me to the King. You will leave

me there, and ride away with the real Princess."

The wolf stamped on the ground. This time he stood there as a maiden so like the Princess Wonderface that even her parents could not have known which was which.

The Prince went into the King's palace and gave up the supposed Princess. He received in exchange the golden-maned horse, bridle and all, and left the King, who was delighted with his bargain. The King asked the Princess for her hand in marriage, and the wedding was announced for the morrow.

The next day lords and ladies of the Court were assembled in the King's throneroom when all at once the supposed Princess turned into a wolf! It gave a dreadful howl, and flew out of the window!

Jan the Prince and the Princess Wonderface, in the meantime, had gone far on their way. When the wolf caught up with them, they were standing near the palace of the King to whom the golden-maned horse had to be given up, in exchange for the Flamebird.

They were sad now, for they had become so fond of their beautiful steed. What could they

do? They must have the Flamebird, for without
it they could not return to Jan's father.

"I see you would like to keep the horse," said
the wolf. "Well, so you shall! I will turn myself
into his likeness, and you, Prince, shall take me to

this King. You will receive the Flamebird, and fly with it and the Princess back to your home." So he stamped his foot once more. There stood a horse so like the one with the golden mane that nobody could tell the difference. The Prince took him to the King, who was delighted. He gave the Prince the Flamebird, cage and all.

Away rode Jan the Prince and the Princess Wonderface. They had not gone far when the wolf overtook them and told them what had happened. He said that the King, charmed with his new steed, gave orders that the Court should follow him to the forest to hunt. They reached the hunting field and the King set off at a gallop in pursuit of a swift-footed deer. Suddenly the King found himself riding a wolf instead of a golden-maned horse! In his fright he fell off, and, while the courtiers were picking him up, the wolf flew away.

Now the wolf took the Prince on his back, and with Princess Wonderface on the horse they soon came to the crossroads where Jan the Prince had first seen the wind-wolf.

"Here we met, Prince, and here we part," said the wind-wolf. "You fed me when I was hungry and I helped you in your need. Good-by, and fare you well, both of you."

With that the wolf flew away, leaving Princess Wonderface and Jan the Prince to travel on the back of the golden-maned horse. Soon they came to the borders of the kingdom over which reigned Jan's father. And whom should they see, resting under a tent in a field, but Jan's two elder brothers! They made a show of greeting Jan and the Princess with joy, but they were secretly jealous when they saw Jan with the Flamebird, the horse, and the beautiful Princess. They invited Jan and the Princess into their tent and regaled them with mead so generously that both soon fell into a deep sleep.

Quickly now they thrust a sharp sword into the body of Jan the Prince. Then they took the

Flamebird, the golden-maned horse, and the Princess to their father's Court.

Jan the Prince lay dead upon the field. Two crows flew down and were just about to light on him when who should come flying along but the wind-wolf!

"Claws off!" he cried, and he seized the smaller of the crows in his jaws.

"Pray, Mr. Wolf, pray spare my child!" cried the old crow. "It is my only one!"

"That I will," said the wolf, "but only if you will fetch me some water from the Eternal Mountain."

This the old crow knew she could do, so she flew away. When she came back she was carrying the water in a small sack. The wolf sprinkled it on the body of Jan the Prince, who opened his eyes.

"You have wakened me from a fine sleep," he said.

"Fine sleep, indeed!" cried the wolf. "It would

have lasted forever but for me. Your brothers killed you, and today the younger is to marry the Princess. But I will help you once more.

"You must take this self-playing pipe and this invisible club and go to your father's palace in disguise. When you are there, blow into the pipe and see what will happen. And don't forget the Princess's ring. The rest I must leave to you." Saying this, he flew away.

The Prince went to the cottage of a peasant he knew and borrowed the working clothes the man wore in the fields. Dressed in them, he slipped into the palace kitchen and discovered that the servants were preparing a great wedding feast.

Jan the Prince then blew into the self-playing pipe. Immediately everything that had life was set a-going. The cook in his apron and cap started prancing. The footmen and kitchenmaids all began dancing, this one with a dish and that one with a platter. There was a shouting and a stamping and a clatter, a hopping and a dancing. As long

as the pipe played, there was no stopping! The
King's marshal came running into the kitchen.
"Cease your playing, O wonderful musician, and
hear the word of the King!" The flute stopped
and all the dancers fell down exhausted. The
marshal announced that the King, who had heard
from his throneroom the wonderful music of the
piper, was inviting the piper to come into his
presence.

"I will go on one condition," said Jan the
Prince. "I wish to drink the health of the bride."

This favor was promised, and Jan was taken to
the King.

"Welcome, O great musician!" cried the King. "We need you here to cheer us. Although this is our son's wedding day and should be a time of rejoicing, everyone has fallen into a deep melancholy. The bride is silent and sad. The Flamebird sings no more, nor does he flash his bright feathers. Golden Mane hangs his head. We beg you, O musician, to play your music and lift our spirits. But first, you shall drink the health of the bride."

A goblet of wine was brought to the supposed piper. As he took it and drank, he dropped into it his half of the ring. He passed the goblet to Princess Wonderface, and, as she drank, the ring touched her lips. She took it, looked at it and then at the piper. She recognized him at once and threw herself into his arms.

The King, too, then knew his son, and embraced him with great joy. Immediately the Flamebird began to carol jubilantly and to flash his brilliant feathers. Golden Mane ran out of his stable neighing with delight. Only the two brothers did not rejoice. They stood looking dumfounded and ashamed.

Jan the Prince now blew into his pipe and at the same time whispered to the invisible club: "Do your work, O Club, and punish the guilty ones."

At the sound of the pipe, everyone began to dance — the King, the bride, the courtiers, and even the Flamebird and Golden Mane. But not all danced with joy, for the invisible club began to rain blows on the backs and shoulders and sides of the two wicked brothers. They dodged and they wriggled and they tried to get out of the way. But, since they could not see what was beating them so soundly, they tried in vain.

At last the piping ceased and everyone stood still. The brothers fell on their knees and begged Jan the Prince to forgive them. This, of course, he did, and there was great rejoicing.

Jan the Prince and the Princess Wonderface joined hands, and their wedding was celebrated that very evening. There was dancing, there was singing, bells were ringing, and people ate and drank to their hearts' delight. I was there, and so I can say how gaily passed the time away.

The Jester Who Fooled a King

A VERY LONG TIME AGO, when King Jan
ruled the kingdom of Poland, there lived in
the royal palace for many years a jester named
Matenko.

Before old age had stiffened his joints and dulled
his wits, Matenko had been the favorite clown in

King Jan's household. He had delighted the King and the Queen, the lords and the ladies, with his antics and his jokes. But now when he performed the nobles yawned. Finally they complained so much that King Jan sent for Matenko to dismiss him.

The old clown approached the King slowly, not only because his bones ached, but because his heart was filled with sorrow. He bent his purple and pink knee, and his respectful but stiff bones cracked loudly. He wished he could die then and there.

King Jan sighed. "My dear old joker," he said sadly, "for a lifetime you have been a merry clown, but age has caught you at last. Put away your gay clothes now, and become a villager." The King sighed once more and straightened his crown. "I've bought a little house in the village for you and your wife, Elzunia. But, I am sorry to say I can give you only a little money to live on. The last Court ball nearly emptied the treasury."

"I understand, Your Majesty," said Matenko. He managed to bow himself out of the royal chamber without too much creaking. He removed his gay clown's suit and his absurd cap with donkey ears, and he laid aside his brightly colored rattle. Then he offered his arm to his wife, Elzunia, and together they made their way to the village to live out their lives in the small cottage the King had given them.

Before long Matenko and Elzunia were penniless, for the King had given them only a few pieces of gold. And there was nothing for the old couple to do. Matenko would willingly have gone to work, but who would give work to an old man who knew nothing except how to act like a fool? They were very hungry, but they had no money for bread. All day and all night they thought of their poverty and were filled with despair.

One night Matenko turned to his wife and asked, "Elzunia, dear, are you asleep?"

"No, Matenko," she answered.

"I have an idea," he said. "Tomorrow you will go to the Queen and tell her that I have died. But before you go, rub both your eyes hard with a raw onion."

"Oh," said Elzunia. "I see."

The next morning she appeared before the Queen with her eyes swollen as if she had been crying long and bitterly.

The Queen asked, sincerely troubled, "Dear Elzunia, why are you grieving so?"

Elzunia answered, sobbing, "Most gracious Queen, last night at eleven o'clock my good husband died. How can I continue to live?"

"Oh, you poor woman!" said the Queen in compassion. "Here, perhaps this will help to give our old jester a decent burial, and you will have something left to live on." And she handed Elzunia her little blue-embroidered purse containing fifty pieces of gold.

When she reached home, Elzunia, laughing, showed Matenko what the Queen had given her.

"It was easy, my love. It's too bad you can't die every day," she said, and giggled when Matenko kissed her.

"Now," he said, "it's your turn to die. To-morrow I'll go to the King and tell him that you have left me desolate." And he kissed his old wife again for luck.

The following day, the old clown twisted his face into an expression of misery and sorrow and set out for the palace. As he bowed before King Jan, he groaned mightily and his shoulders shook with sobs.

"Oh, my poor old joker!" said the King with the utmost compassion. "What misfortune has come to you?"

Matenko wiped his eyes. "Gracious Majesty, my dear wife entrusted her soul to God only this morning. She is lying dead in our little cottage, and I am all alone in the world and penniless."

"My poor clown," said the King gently, "take this purse of gold and do not grieve so desperately.

But I know how I would feel, should anything happen to my Queen."

When Matenko reached the cottage, he poured the money from the purse onto the table and found that the King had given him two hundred pieces of gold.

"My dear wife," said Matenko, putting his arm around her, "the King's sympathy, as you see, is worth more than the Queen's. We have two hundred and fifty pieces of gold, so we won't starve for a little while. But we'd better lie down and pretend we're dead, in case the King and Queen come to find out if we really are."

And with much giggling on the part of Elzunia and much chuckling on the part of Matenko, each put a thick coating of flour on the other's face. They lay down on the bare floor and covered themselves carefully with a white muslin sheet.

"Stop laughing," said Matenko, trying to compose his features into a likeness of death.

"*You* stop," retorted Elzunia. "You're making

me shake off all my flour! Stop!" she exclaimed.

And there they lay quietly with one candle burning at their heads and one candle burning at their feet.

At the palace, in the meantime, a fine argument was going on. The Queen declared that the old jester was dead, whereas the King insisted that it was not the clown but his wife who had died. They argued back and forth and got nowhere. At last the King suggested that they go to the cottage and see for themselves. The Queen agreed, and they summoned the royal coach.

At Matenko's house they found the old jester and his wife lying on the floor under a white shroud, with candles for the dead burning at their heads and their feet. King Jan and his Queen looked at each other, and tears filled their eyes, for they had loved their old clown. They prayed for the departed souls of Matenko and Elzunia. The Queen wiped her eyes and the King coughed loudly.

As they were about to leave the little house, King Jan said to the Queen, "I wonder which of the two old folks died first."

"In all honesty, my beloved King," replied the jester from the floor, "my wife died first, but I was dead before."

"Oh, you rascals!" The King choked and laughed. "Get up immediately and tell me what this trickery means!"

Matenko was reluctant to tell how poor he and Elzunia had been, but King Jan understood at once and realized that he was to blame. He gave Matenko another purse of two hundred pieces of gold. And he asked him to promise never again to use his wits dishonestly.

The old clown promised.

Favorite Fairy Tales
Retold by
Virginia Haviland

TOLD IN ENGLAND

TOLD IN FRANCE

TOLD IN GERMANY

TOLD IN IRELAND

TOLD IN NORWAY

TOLD IN POLAND

TOLD IN RUSSIA

TOLD IN SCOTLAND

TOLD IN SPAIN